Marie Désires is a French Caribbean poet
from London. Growing up in a colourful
family, she uses life and experience to
influence her writing.

Her other works include *Monochromatic* and
Mother.

Contents

Also by Marie Désires

monochromatic

Mother: This Is Not A Story.

In Sight Of Others.

Come, call and collect a tale of deus et ire

From which acid tears reflect the course of mortal desire

A mother's tale reborn, under histories unfurled

With childlike wonder, we kneel at her weary hearth

Thus, into the Caraïbes we head, under colonial banners we sail

As fears ignite in the present dead, following tragedy's bloody trail

Staggered histories reveal the sordid madras colours

That which all parties seek conceal when in sight of others

i.   la madinina

If you should ever go to the West Indies, to the colonies of
the French Antilles, you will find beyond the islands green,
sands of time, sprung beneath cool verdant leaves of
flowers, bloomed in the fragrant past that form its
histories;

You may hear of the silent cries that warble and wail under
each crashing wave, echoing loud under its boundaries
lined, the rising moans of boats overloaded, sunk, under
the fraught ropes of crates and chains, clanging in unison
under the warm setting sun;

You could count with each island breath held, the
movements of the natives, the Arawaks, the Caribs and the
Békés baked into soft clay, breaking bread with the dough
of one forced to knead, trading in the blood given by those
whose hands shred horrors, housed in the safe comforts of
peoples made to kneel;

Should you come visit the fertile lands, there are things you
must first know, for secrets held in fists of tribal bandes
reveal the truth of those who came before, singing of the
unsightly and uncanny, in which humans bought are freed
to

dally and dance with the supernatural;

Should you stay, the locals may just talk, singing verses of death, the sweet riches of immortality swollen under eerie gold, and the mysteries of the island call, beckoning and delighting in the chaos of charges brought to heel;

You may just witness the strength of souls forgotten under the heat of yesterday's cries and yesteryear's fears, realised and made to fall under the weight of colloquial spirits and ghouls sought by hosts left behind each town beholden to its own spectre, its own tale and toll.

ii.   mami mordu

My grandmother was one such spirit:

Mami Mordu, the 'Bitten One' they called her in Madinina, made mad by the moon, rocking under its gleam as if embraced in a tendre, swaying to a strain swept up and away by the faintest gust, carried to where she'd stay, trickling down from their source up in the mountains;

Hers was the air about her, and hers became the night as I knelt by her feet, and there I stayed, as she caressed my hair, her gaze strung sweet on the sky, her heart in her arms, embraced and interlaced with mine;

Mami was but a frail thing, a centennial veteran serving still as a sentinel of the Lesser guard, bones as brittle as the sugar snap flexing beneath peach fuzz and honey cannelle, electric spice in her hair, wiry strands blanched by coarse sea salt and tropical rays;

In her eyes I saw mine, walnut brown cracked and cradled by folds of age and wear, clouded with stars of lucidity I could only see in my reflection, her smiles spoke of unbidden joys and smitten tranquilities, her laugh a jeweller's delight and rarest commodity, bestowed on blush cheeks with a soft kiss;

It was there at her feet I learned, from her rocking perch she taught me in the hushed tones of her voice, likened to a lark's song, of the worlds beyond mortal eyes, wherein the bounds of morality buckle under the merged form of gluttonous desire and love is sacrificed at the altar of the masses;

It began under the sun's fading glow, on the dimpled sands of the golden beach, on rough knitted rugs made from spun coconut hairs, crude and coir, her wrinkled hand in my dense cotton coils, she said to me:

iii.   ti'pierre

There is an islet a little way away, so small you could circle it in a matter of hours, so small as to hardly qualify, that stands between this island and the next. It is known to the locals as Ti' Pierre, 'the little rock', an isle frequented by the flocking tourists yet left untouched by those who know of its past.
You see, ma p'tite, there once lived a small commune that teemed with life; theirs was a secluded village, nestled among ancient trees, with thatch huts made from plantain leaves and palm tree posts and branches, hacked and woven into communal homes.

Every morning, the men swam out with roped nets and hand carved canoes, as the women nursed the young and the ill, and the youth cared for the elderly. For these were not the savages you hear of in the records of our history, the so-called flesh-eaters who gave us our name, non ma p'tite, these were the last of the Arawaks, the original settlers, driven out of the main islands by the Caribs. Many men, young and old, had been slaughtered at their hands, many more women enslaved et violée, made heavy with their bâtards and made to work.

Desperate to protect his people, le cacique took their last goat kid out to the sea and offered it out to la mer as a sacrifice.
Tu vois, ma p'tite, they understood the power of the ocean, the spirits that dwell within its depths. They gave

thanks when the western current filled their traps, and the eastern returned their nets laden, and when the summer storms blew around, their ancestors reached out through the waters to warn them.

And so, the tribe moved into the deserted isle, blessedly avoided by the Caribs, who believed the isle inhabited by demons. Ah oui, des démons- these were not the red men with horns, non, non. These were the shapeshifters, the ghouls that quietly steal into your home and te détruit from the inside out.
As was their nature, they brought with them two Caribs, young sisters who had been held prisoner but taken as wives by le grand cacique, the chieftain, who had lost many sons to the Caribs.

Mami's voice trails off, hissing sand whittling down to a soft hum; together we watch as the sun dips beneath near motionless waves; in the budding darkness, bullish croaks break into the stillness, startling the night; in spite of the fallen sun, Mami's arms are warm, balmy to the touch, her hands in mine, her flittering pulse a soothing drum to which her words seemed to beat:

Many years passed and all was well; their crops flourished, the sickly grew strong and in time, both sisters grew enceinte, and the shaman to was called upon to reveal their fates.

All drew round the women, fond as they had become of their newest tribemates, eager to hear what the spirits had to say. Preparations were made, nouveau zemis carved from driftwood and etched in stone slabs, each figure bearing the face of their deities. Feathers and face paints made from crushed coral and clay were adorned, and the sisters bore ritualistic markings on their swollen middles.

Soon came the hour according to the stars, for they read the stars in their own way ma p'tite, and it seemed determined that day, that the sisters give birth together, for their children carried the same dates, down to the hour. They were prophesised to live as great warriors, born with the strength of le cacique's fallen sons, born to protect the islanders; they seemed a gift, as if from the gods themselves, but it was not to be.

When it came time to deliver, the sisters were nowhere to be found.

'What happened to them, mami?'

Gone, cher, parti, let mami tell you:

Some say the Caribes stole them back across the waters, others say they drowned trying to escape les démons, mais ma p'tite, Mami knows better- the devil got a hold of them there, the women and their sweet babes; he slipped through them spirits just as the shaman called, and grasped them tight. By the time even le cacique realised what had happened, their spirit was gone, and in its place remained a shell, hollow and rung with the foreign motionlessness in their wombs.

The Arawak tradition is that they died naturally, dans un accident, but their bodies were never found, and no matter how intensely the shaman scried, the stars held their tongue, the ancestors kept leur silence also.

What was noticed, was the disappearance a fishing net, unhooked from its place by the canoes. It seemed very much a mystery that would haunt them forever, yet as the skies darkened and the clouds rumbled their protests, secrets threatened to reveal themselves.

I'm sure you can imagine, ma p'tite', the isle mourned its losses, not only their former female companions, but more specifically les enfants perdu, the young warriors promised to deliver them from the Caribes' burgeoning zeal; with time came the inevitable, an evolution of the mind to follow the body.

Where there once was fear, grew a new boldness, and with the growing presence of Spaniards, a new faith, that marked the start of the end for the Arawaks.

I was tangled, my wares ensnared by Mami's bitten tale, and the dim light of the stars.

'Why did the devil take their souls, mami?'

iv.   ti bonom

Tu sais ma p'tite, le diable est le mal incarné, and evil that
pure cannot be understood any more than I could
comprehend the works of the Lord.

What I do know is what happened to another young soul
when his parents invoked the wrong spirit- ti bonom, they
called him, 'little man', from the house just over that hill,
there. Just beyond those trees, the valley dips into the base
of the mountain, just beyond which lay his family's sugar
cane farm, thick stalks protruding from the ground like
incense sticks of hollowed sticky sweetness.

Every morning, avant l'école, he'd walk along the dirt road
to the crosswalk, take a right and follow the banana trees
along till he reached the school building. Back then, it was
more a classroom than anything, but we all crammed in
together, the elders with the youngers, and grew to know
each other by name.

 He was a year or two older than me, yet barely stood eye
to eye, and his clothes, a thin shirt and cotton shorts hung
off his wiry form, revealing knobbed elbows and bony
shoulders; Well, ma p'tite, it had gotten around town that
his parent's company had run into some trouble for quite
some time- overused equipment and hurricane storms had
led to damaged crops and spoilt batches so often, they
were losing business.

Now, in the village, as you know, there was a little church where we go to confess, light our candles and leave them to stand under la Vierge Marie's solemn gaze. I did it with my mother and yours, and now you too carry on the tradition-

'We cross ourselves, grab a candle, offer a prayer of thanks and a Hail Mary, cross ourselves again and place it to burn on the candlestick holder.'

Exactement. As a child, we went every afternoon before heading home, the other pupils and Ti Bonom. Well, ma p'tite, on this day, Bonom carried with him a candle from home; it was a large red thing, with a black ribbon tied around it in with a sailor's knot. His mother had given it to him, and though she never admitted where she'd conjured, it had voodoo's dark scent along its wick.
Still, he crossed himself, said a Hail Mary and placed it with the others. Hardly an hour had passed when he complained of a headache:

it began as a tickle,
a sudden force came over him, his ears,
a trickling weight that dripped,
oozing a thunderous buzz that swarmed about him,
across his head, and more:
'kill them!' he cried, fingers grasping down towards his heart,

at the air, his ears, reddening shells;
as it reached his eyes, he began to scream,
his desperation a thickening smog-
a purpling haze as the pain drifted;

clawing at his face, further still-
his face had swollen up from crud bitten nails carvings,
his lips held stiffly agape, his tongue blistering red welts in
his mouth,
cracked, parched, choking him,
as his cries became garbled moans,
sounds of a wounded animal

Crois-mois ma p'tite, before the sun had set that very day,
he was paralyzed, de la tête aux pieds, frozen in his body,
unable to do more than open his eyes. His papa came
down to the church and carried him in while we waited for
the nearest médecin to come over.

A white man came up the church steps, bag in hand and
swept his way inside. You know what he was, ma p'tite?
Un Béké, descended from the settlers themselves, come
down from their maison de ville to investigate. Of course
he found nothing, une gripe, he called it, a very serious
strain, had he had any illnesses before and the like; he
could only see what his mortal eyes saw, and even that was
blurry from des préjugés.

Non, it was le guérisseur, schooled in the arts of herbal
charms and spiritual healings, who saw which devil had
grasped his soul in hand -

He was a young man yet older even than me ma p'tite,
over millennia according to legend, in a well-built frame.

He was known as Papis Tourés, the 'Twisted One', for he
had met La Diablesse, spurned her seduction and walked
away unscathed but for his heart-

torn from the hidden cavity of his chest, splayed out of his
torso, beating each pulse as if out of his chest.

To most he was the local spiritualist, but to those who had
opened eyes, his incantations opened the bounds between
realms.

When he examined Ti Bonom, he forbade us from
touching him as he rubbed anise and cinnamon into his
skin; his fingers and toes were dipped in the blood of a
black lamb, and splayed across his torso, upon his head he
places a wreath of coconut fibres.

He was left alone in the church crypt for a sen 'night as the
red candle continued to burn, its wax ran rouge, but
hardened black as offerings were made to appease the
spirit that held him captive.

His parents sacrificed their last sugar cane crop, watching
as its rum rained upon their son, onto the stone slabs
below. On that last day, cher, we saw him stumble out with
his parents as Papis saged his path. That was the last we
saw him, blank eyed, trembling as his parents led him
away. They were gone in a matter of days, for fear the
spirit would return to claim the rest of him.

It was angered, tu vois: you cannot appease both the Lord and the spirits: there isn't enough soul to go round.

Mami fell silent once more, and closed her eyes and under the site of the full moon above, she stilled, bathing under light; That night, we returned to the seclusion of her home, and by the fireplace, I took my place, seated by her feet she sank into the cushioning of her seat.

'Please, won't you tell me more, mami?'

'Je suis fatigue, ma p'tite, I will finish l'histoire des Arawaks in the morning.'

I left her to rest and contented myself with the creole fables on the nightstand by her bed.

It was there I learnt more of the Twisted One:

v.   papis tourés

       If you should ever go to the West Indies, look
beyond the islands green, and gaze

up at a galaxy glowing ever golden above, sculpting stars
under night's shrouded

cover, free forming and evolving in a language forgotten
by most, but not Papis;

His is the island charm, with hips that speak with crisp
fluency, the language of the

 natives, a calypso swing, riding the electric hum as he slips
into trance, awoken

 only by the morning cries, as he shakes off the weight of
the evening, of dreams

inhabited by his blanket sprite;

His eyes burn like coal lumps, smouldering as he fixes his
stare on you, a mahogany

 mass looming over you as he glides through, dark skin
simmering under the sun's

 broil, his hair thick woollen ropes of charcoal grey, baring
buzzed edges and

 naked necks glistening with beaded sweat;

His youthful visage throws human senses into disarray
with each careful smile,

 canines bared, pearl white, cunning as a crocodile
presenting for inspection, a

predatorial grin strategically placed, welcome innocent
eyes, as his hands reach out,

claws out, each wrist adorned with the silver etching of
aged time;

He is a spectre to the human mind, a delightful mystery to
the roaring crowds that

 line the gates of the netherworlds, where he forsook one
flittering form for another-

 Ansi, Papa des Bois, ansi Papa Legba;

 His garb is loose fitting, red, black and green, couleurs des
espirits that he serves,

 Blood, brow and the earth enslaved and freed, natural
liberation and a decadent

spring as if born from the very plants and trees he coaxes
spice and magic from,

 upon his head beaded charm of boar tusks and flowers, a
piece of madinina

 entrusted in his care.

Such were the images that lulled me to sleep.

vi.   sirène

I awoke to the gentle lulling of the tide retreating,
soft laps that curled in on itself in a coquettish
scuttle; I could hear mami's deep snuffs as she
turned over trying to locate the 'cool' spot. I threw
on a light robe and crept past her room, eager to
feel the rising sun on my skin before the heat truly
set in.

I sunk my toes deeper into the fine white granules,
careful to avoid the raised mounds where snapper
crabs no doubt lay in wait. The ground dampened
to a soft squelch as I reached the exposed seabed.
Looking around, I spotted a few other early risers,
eagerly shuffling sand rifts and digging for
mussels, a few cocoa brown kids splashing around
residual pools, dragging seaweed clumps around
like streamers, fluffy heads a briny grey from the
mud and salt.

I trudged further, the warm slurry creeping higher
on my legs. Just around the cliff face was a cave
entrance usually inaccessible during high tide. I
slipped through the narrow passageways till they
gave way to the open sky and clear rock pools I
remembered from my childhood. A quick swish
confirmed it was warm enough for a quick soak,
and I hastily undressed before sinking in, wriggling

my arms about till I found the hidden boulder that made for a seat.

I watched as the drying sand rinsed off in the swirling pool before I submerged my head in completely.

With my eyes closed, all there was for me to do was feel -

the current running over my exposed skin,

the bobbing flow of seaweed strands and they flickered past my back,

my breasts floating, weightless,

the sensitivity of my every nerve as I hung there,

frozen -

unbidden, I thought of one of mami's many stories, of Mama Dlo, the sea witch who abducts the souls of lone swimmers and fishermen in exchange for their lifelong servitude;

I could hear her voice in my head, calling me out of the water, promising more tales while she'd brush the knots from my hair, pocketing them; as I reached out to take her hand, I felt a vice take

hold my ankle, encircling my leg, sharpened points
dug into the flesh of thigh and jerk-

I broke through the surface with a choked gasp
and made for the stone ledge, frantically grasping
at my leg. My arm came away clasping the rotting
remains of a net.

The sight didn't slow my heart's pounding beats as
I flung it from the pool, peering down expecting
to see the skeletal remains of le cacique's sister
wives. My own face peered back at me, startling a
shaky laugh from me, and I made to climb out
before I noticed a figure in the corner.

vii.   la dame du nord

The woman was also draped in a robe, only hers was a thick, heavy material, made from heavy drapery that reached the ground and trailed in the puddles. Her hair was wrapped in a cloth headdress, yet she hardly moved, even as it sat at an odd perch on her head, as though waiting to slide off at the slightest movement. Her lips were painted rouge, her eyes were unusually bare. For a moment, neither of us spoke, until she came forward, and handed me my robe,

'Will you not dress?' she asked me, and I hastily drew on the dampening fabrics like an errant schoolgirl, my eyes on her while she glanced towards the cave entrance.

'The tide won't come in for a while,' she turned to me, hazel eyes flashing. 'Would you mind keeping me company?' As if sensing my disbelief, she added, 'I brought lunch,' and gestured towards a hidden alcove where I could make out the top of wicker basket.

I found myself nodding before I could understand, and we sat by the rock pool as she fished out all manners of food from her basket. We ate in silence for a time, and I watched her as she ate, her eyes trailed on the ground in front of her as if it were presenting her with something only she could see.

Eventually she wiped her mouth and turned that unflinching stare towards me.

'I wish to tell you a story,' she started, holding up a hand when I started to speak. 'Please, I only have the courage to say this once.'

I held my tongue and nodded in support. For what was a story between lunch companions?

> She stood and walked to the other side of the cavern, removing her outer robe, revealing a fabulous ensemble of white flowing sleeves and the heavy ruffled skirts of traditional madras attire dyed choking red and green, stuttering white lines in the tale-tale style of batik art, that fell in waves to just above her ankles.
> She wore strings of golden beads, wound once, twice, thrice about her neck and upper torso that rubbed against each other with a rhythmic chack chack chack of pearls clacking together.
> Around her ankles were two thick bracelets, made of chiselled bones blanched brilliant white by sea and sun; hooked into the heavy bands were silver coins, now freed from the heavy robe, that clinked with her every step.
> From my seat, I saw faces imprinted on some, snake and ram heads on the other. Charms, ma p'tite, heard whispered through the air, my grandmother's voice echoing in the cavernous dome.

I fingered my own charm- the small silver crucifix resting at the base of my neck, the letters INRI etched in tiny lettering; meant to protect my soul from blasphemous spirits.

Before me, la dame took position, one foot raised about the other as her arms crossed her face in quick jerks, as if pulled by stringed tendons, involuntary but helpless to control it. She began moving, one foot always in the air, bursts of movement that clinked and chacked with every bounce. As she moved, halting here, and twirling there, there came to be music, a rhythmic pulse accompanying her crude instruments, as the slap of bare feet on wet sand and stone began to tell a story. It was then she began to sing:

viii.   la diablesse

'I come from up north

A village just beyond

Hidden from the city

Up in the cracks of the mountain curve

Every morning, we climb

In pitch black and red lines,

Scaling above the horizon

Singing mbale! mbale!

The sound of our ancestors

mbale! mbale!

They answer in the night.

She sings in Martinican creole, the words clacking into one another, soft sound, hard sounds tumbling together in song, a fixture of colonial histories that spring from her without hesitation, in all the confidence of a tongue reclaimed:

In the summer months, the land thrives and pulses

Babies bloom and flowers give birth

Everyone sings and dances with merry might

For in the winter crops are made barren

As the mountain swallows its tongue

mbale! mbale!

We eat and make merry

mbale! mbale!

They eat with us too.

The chief leads us in strength

Six sons and daughters

Seven generations made strong

Ice in their veins

Power in their loins

mbale! mbale!

Where he leads the flock follow

mbale! mbale!

They grow with us too.

The chief's wife falls ill, a state no man can heal

We call to our ancestors, in whose help we désir

They send to us Papis Lou

The twisted man

He tells them to fast, for la Diablesse is coming

mbale! mbale!

When she comes blood must run

mbale! mbale!

It runs through us too.

Nine days the town fasted, from the young to the old

And the chief's wife awoke

Day ten, the town celebrated, ate dates and drank rum

For it seemed the end of their plight

But Papis remained, for his task was not through

La Diablesse appeared in the night

With her a golden ram

Who slaughtered every child,

From where they nursed in their mother's arms

That night mbale! mbale!

Was their chant of pain

mbale! mbale!

They grieved with us too.

The winter months drew near, and all around the town

Bellies grew round in a bursts of new life

Together, they rebuilt in the wake of children lost

All but the chief's wife

Whose womb remained sealed tight.

As the mountains swallowed their tongue

The chief's field was left barren

Seven generations burned

He cried in the darkness

As Papis Lou watched with twisted eyes

mbale! mbale!

mbale! mbale!

Into the empty night

mbale! mbale!

They turned from him too.

The chief sought the shaman, who led him to Ti'Pierre

There he spent a month in cleansing

Sleeping in the wild, eating the earth's raw offerings

Until at last he heard them

mbale! mbale!

He returned home once more

mbale! mbale!

They returned with him too.

The chief's wife grew round but the babe didn't survive

The boy was offered to Mama Dlo,

Who turned it away

Still, they tried again

And the chief's strength began to weaken

As seven summers passed them by

mbale! mbale!

As his wife called out to the ancestors

mbale! mbale!

They called out to her too.

Papis appeared at their door,

Took the bones of their first born.

He tossed them before the ancestors

'La nuit blanche' was called:

Each night spent apart, every night in another's bed

As the chief's wife returned sated,

He could barely perform

Till the day his wife returned to him

Glowing with another man's labour.

mbale! mbale!

He cursed their very name

mbale! mbale!

They cursed him too.

He sought la Diablesse

He returned to Ti'Pierre and fasted for many adays,

Running through empty woods

Growing sharp and sickly till at last they meet:

So tall as to brush her hair on the palm leaves

Pupils cut like that of a goat in eyes glowing white

with the fading rays of the moon

Her lips wet with blood that dripped even from her hands

In her hand a beating heart of a lover sought

Her hair long, an ebony curtain, that moved about her

even in the absence of a breeze, brushing the tops of feet

cloven, hooves

mbale! mbale!

His ancestors cried

But he could not hear them through the hush of her voice.

She offered him a bite from her heart

Which he accepted with no other thought but hunger

A pulsing beating desire that overwhelmed him

And he fainted at her feet

He awoke in his bed

His wife in his arms

Her womb was heavy, as was he

And without thought, he pushed in

And rutted with mindless abandon

Till his hunger of years was at last sated

He closed his eyes and slept

With the taste of blood and honey in his mouth.

He dreamt of his children

Running in the mountains with the other lost babes

Dancing as they did that night so long ago

His wife appeared besides him, two swaddles in hand

He glanced down and caught sight of cloven feet

And thrust them from her arms

His kids stood on shaken feet, and he watched

As his wife bent over to let them suckle at her teats

mbale! mbale!

He heard in the distance

and caught sight of Papis across the field

mbale! mbale!

He gazed down at his feet

mbale! mbale!

The chief looks down to see

a giant ram

with horns of burnished gold

trampling his kid to death

with heavy hooves

as ebony as the night

mbale! mbale!

He awakens to find his seat

A flood in strands woven red

Blood drips from his hands and tears from his eyes

For his wife lays dead

As the spirits cry

MBALE! MBALE!

he cries with them too

ix.   d'être humain

La dame lets out a full-throated scream and
collapses at my feet as the cave echoes mbale!
mbale!

It is a word I have heard mami cry in her sleep
and utter in praise, a call to the spirits that watch
over us. It lingers on the tip of my tongue as I
rush out of the cave, abandoning la dame to her
fate as I run back to the shelter of mami's
embrace, a chorus of mbale! mbale! following me
home.

Mami is already swinging in her hamac as the sun
crests over the treetops, familiar fibres in her hand
as calloused fingers weave patterned sheets from
dried palm tree leaves, an echo of songs from
generations past. She says nothing as I rush to my
place at her side, but her eyes carry a knowing
glint.

'What did you see out there ma p'tite?'

I rest my head on my knee as she pauses her work,
hands trembling with the wear of age, as they do
when they are no longer occupied. Delicate fingers
traced the planes of my face with feather-light
sweeps.

'To be human is to seek more than you have. To desire that which is unobtainable, to fight that which is determined and reject what is incomprehensible to us. It is why the spirits linger- we always have need of them, to grant us the answers we want, and the not the pre-ordained desires of any one being, divine or otherwise.'

Her eyes found mine.

'The heavens bear witness, et le diable tempts us for his pleasure; but make no mistake, child. We are the maker of our own downfall.'

'I promised you and end to that story,' she rasps, and her hand pause their movements.

'When the sisters learnt of their children's fate…

The younger sister, whose Kalinago name was Bataca, rushed to offer a prayer of thanks to the gods, and pray for their safe delivery, for she had been young when the Arawaks stole her away with them, just thirteen, and had no fixed memories of her life as a Carib. However, her sister, Calibishie, who was now twenty, still bore resentment towards le cacique, as she had been promised to a young handsome man from their tribe whom she had loved, but he had died trying to protect her moments before her capture. Alors, ma p'tite, upon learning that her child would be a warrior for the same people who she'd come to hate, she began to plot her escape.

Every day in the weeks leading up to her disappearance, she'd take a walk by the edges of the beach, where Carib scouts were often sighted and raise her head in false prayers. Soon, her lover's uncle spotted her as she brushed her hair out by the sea and rushed over to see her. The two soon fell into a passionate affair and made plans to run away together mais it proved harder to find the time to get away as the due date grew near, and more eyes were placed upon the sisters. Knowing they could never be together while the cacique awaited his child, Calibishie plotted to kill her sister and pretend the babe was her own before escaping.

And that is exactly what she did; enlisting the help of Audel, her young servant girl, she lured her sister away under the pretence of offering praise to the sea, and as Bataca bent in worship, her lover sprang up from the water and drowned her sister as she watched. The babe was cut out, swathed in blankets and given to Audel, to pass off as her mistress' child, as its true mother was wrapped in a net laden with rocks and quietly sunken in the middle of the sea.

As Audel disappeared into the dense brush, Calibishie felt her own pains start, and within the

hour, both babes had arrived. It seemed ma p'tite,
that at least one spirit had seen the injustice of it
all and deigned intercede; let it be a lesson to you,
my dear- there is only so many times you can call
on a spirit, even in pretence, before they actually
appear.

Thus, unbeknownst to them, Mama Dlo reached
out and touched Bataca's child as soon as she
emerged from her mother's womb, submerged in
her salted waters. She eased Calibishie's own
delivery and watched as the murderers made off
with the child, softly paddling away over her
doorstep, celebrating their escape.
The arrogance of the moment struck her, and with
an indignant gust, overturned their escape,
dragging them to join her at its ocean depths, the
new babe cooing in her selkie arms.

'I thought you said the devil took their souls,
mami?'

He did indeed, ma p'tite. Is this the work of the
Lord?

'No, of course now, but I thought you meant he
killed them.'

He did indeed ma p'tite- he took them both the moment Bataca gave her last breath. In that moment, Calibishie lost her humanity, and that is all he needs. He cares not about your flesh, your worldliness, except for where he can use it to destroy you. Now stop interrupting, you'll make me forget.

x.   la foule

Calibishie's plan proceeded as she'd hoped, cher- no one found her or her wayward lover, and the Arawaks had at least one warrior child; only, when the swatches were fully drawn back for the first time, there was a collective gasp at the sight that greeted them- for the babe was a girl.

A sweet thing, of mild and gentle temperament, with skin and hair as pale as coconut flesh, and just as delicate.

Most of her childhood days were spent indoors, as the tropical sun seared her flesh, and she needed water near constantly ma p'tite, or she'd collapse right where she stood! At first, the Arawaks coddled her, sheltering her every move as they'd never seen anything quite like her, and thought her divinity itself.
When they saw she was much too fragile for even the simplest of tasks- peeling bananas, or weaving baskets and ropes, which left her hands blistering red and swollen for days- they began to fear her.

For who was she, cher, to have appeared so suddenly, on the day so divinely marked a sworn day of reckoning. She became a blight from the gods, a sign that they had faulted in some way.

So they cast their troubles up onto her, believing her to be a living talisman, made to carry their disease, their misdeeds, their shame and suffer in their stead.

She was left out in the sun on its hottest day, with only the animals' trough to drink from, and overripe plantain to nourish her; not even her father, would house her at night, believing her to carry spectres within her body.

Le cacique had one other child born to him on this island, another little girl, sired but a few days after Bataca's child, born a week later. Her name was Barica, after the young Carib who he had grown to love and mourned terribly. To the pale child, Barica was a symbol of everything she should have been; her name, one spoken with reverence and affection, a final crown upon her mahogany brow.

She had no name, as even from birth, her father could not find a place for her.

Barica was warned not to play with her sister yet couldn't resist, being so close in age; after her birth, many avoided pregnancy for fear of producing a child of her affliction. The two would sneak out at night, when the moon was at its brightest, and play for hours beneath its light. It was on one such night that they snuck out to swim along the shore, when they were swept up in

a current and brought out to sea. They clung to
each other as the waves grew rougher, until they
found a small rocky mound protruding from them
to grab a hold of. There, they stayed for hours
until dawn brought with it the early fishers in their
canoes.

They carried little Barica home and vowed to
return for the young girl. Perhaps they had at one
time thought to save the pale child, cher, but she
was left there as the sun rose to its peak and began
its descent. When dusk came, the girl sought to
unclench her fingers, to let go and sink into the
cooling waters, but something within her refused
to give up.

At last came her father on a lone canoe. The girl
could barely open her eyes, the skin around them
blistered and swollen, yet she tried to anyway, if
only for the sight of her father coming to save her.

Upon seeing her en vie, he simply rowed back the
way he came. You see, cher, he only came so he
could confirm she was dead, as he had hoped.
That was too much for the young child, who
opened her eyes unto the moon and begged for
death.

Instead, it was Mama Dlo who greeted the child as
a dear friend and carried her to shore under the
moon's knowing gaze. There she apologised for
touching her as a babe and inflicting this cursed

life upon her- she'd only wanted to comfort the cries of a motherless child. Mami tells her of her mother's fate, as I tell you now, and grants the pale child a gift: Should she ever wish to leave this world to its fate and come home, she need only make one small sacrifice.

Tu vois, ma p'tite, when Mama Dlo took Calibishie's child, another was needed to replace the upset balance of twin fates. Thus, when le cacique gave his second daughter the name that should have been hers, he restored that balance and allowed the island to thrive, despite the Caribs awaiting them just over the sea that separated them.

'Alors, the only thing that kept them safe was Barica's name? I find that hard to believe, mami'

Non, non- they lived only because, for all their atrocities towards her, the young girl never had a reason to forsake them. She'd had no one and nowhere else to go until she was truly forsaken and held by Mama Dlo.

When Barica slipped out of her home that very night, desperate to find her sister, she found her right there on that sandy shore, waiting for her. She told her stories of a realm where they could play forever and never be separated. Overjoyed to see her alive and well, Barica followed her blindly into Mama Dlo's open arms.

As for the Arawaks, ma p'tite – within moments of the sisters' disappearance, a strange thrall took hold of them that night.

When the Caribs appeared on the island the next morning, coming to investigate the disappearance of their fellow brother all those years ago, they found every inch of Ti'Pierre littered with the slaughtered bodies of men, women and children, the likes of which they'd never seen.

If there were any doubts about the shapeshifters, these were swiftly assuaged, and they vowed to never step foot on that island again.

xi.

sous la lune

I left mami mordu there swinging softly in the breeze of the waking day, beneath the trance of her words we left the tale.

I returned to my mother's home that evening under the moon's watchful gaze.

It seemed brighter, rounder, full on the highs of the past few nights, winking down at me. I basked in its glorious ray as I prepared for bed, my head flowing with my mami's words.

If you lay beneath the moon's light, when it is at its roundest, it will grab a hold of you forever.

As I glanced up once more, I sent up a silent plea;

May I rest forever more under the sweetness of the moon's light. And may I be as bright as the stars that dance above, as bitten as my mami's words, and flourish in the aftermath. May the wisdom of ages be mine and more, forever more.

With these words in minds, I lay down and slept. What I saw in the night who knows, for I won't say.

At least, not today.

But should you wish to know what more I heard and saw from The Bitten One, you may have to step foot on the isle of Ti'Pierre for yourself.

monochromatic

It is our individual experiences that colour our
lives, that inspire us to create and share with the
world. They define who we are, distinguish us from
the others. But for all the colours that there are in
the world, perhaps they aren't so different in black
and white.

MOTHER.

Life and love in ludic poetry.

Printed in Great Britain
by Amazon